and the Donkey

BRIAN WILDSMITH

One fine morning the miller decided to take his donkey to market and sell him.

FABLE

The Miller, the Boy and the Donkey

BASED ON A FABLE BY LA FONTAINE

The Miller, the Boy

OXFORD
UNIVERSITY PRESS

So he and his boy
went out into the
field to catch him.

They took with them some carrots which the donkey loved to eat. Sure enough when he saw the carrots the donkey came trotting towards them.

When he had eaten the carrots they took him to the mill and brushed his coat and polished his hooves and combed his mane. He looked so smart and clean the miller decided to carry him to market to save him from dirtying his feet on the way.

They had not gone very far before they
met a farmer.

He burst out laughing when he saw them. "How silly you are," he cried. "Fancy carrying a donkey! Why he should be carrying you, not you carrying him."

The miller did not like to be laughed at,

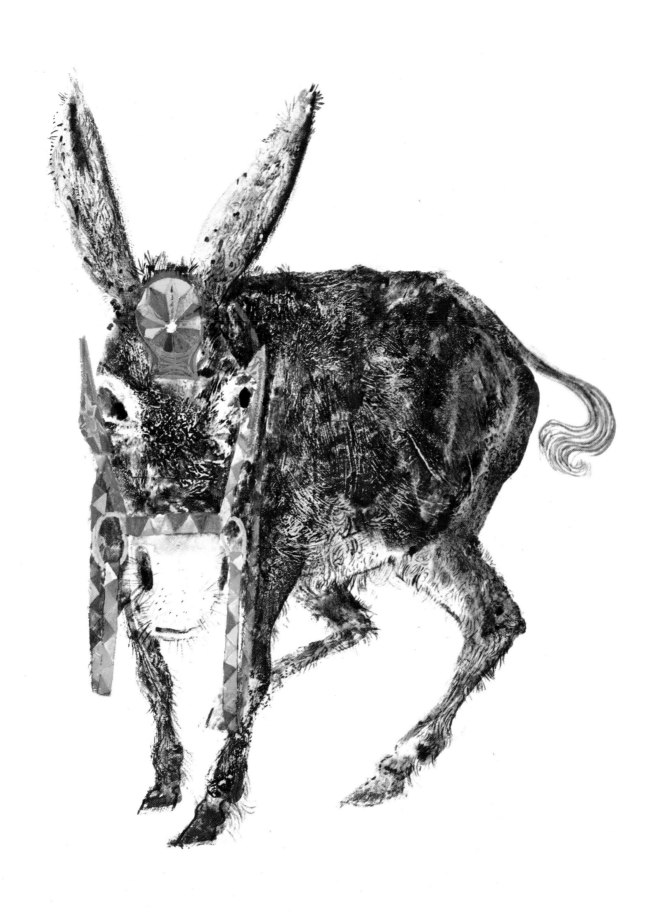

so he made the donkey start walking.

Then the boy began to feel tired and the miller
lifted him on to the donkey's back.

A little further on they met three merchants who were angry when they saw the boy riding while the miller walked.

"Why you lazy lad," they said. "Get down from the donkey and let the old man ride."

The miller made the boy get down and he

himself climbed on to the donkey's back. But it was very hot and the boy soon became tired again.

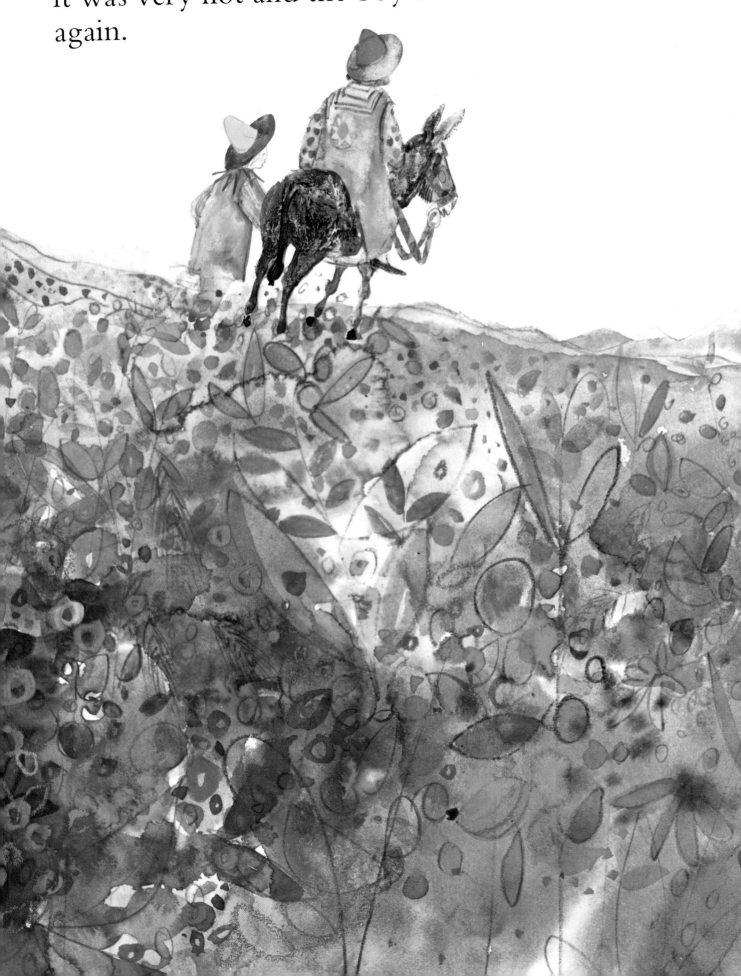

After a while they met three girls. "Shame on you master," they called out. "How can you ride at ease while your poor boy limps so wearily behind?"

So the miller told the boy to climb up behind him and they both rode on the donkey.

Before long they saw a priest standing outside his church. He rebuked the miller sternly. "It is cruel for both of you to ride on the back of this little animal. Have you no pity for such a faithful beast?"

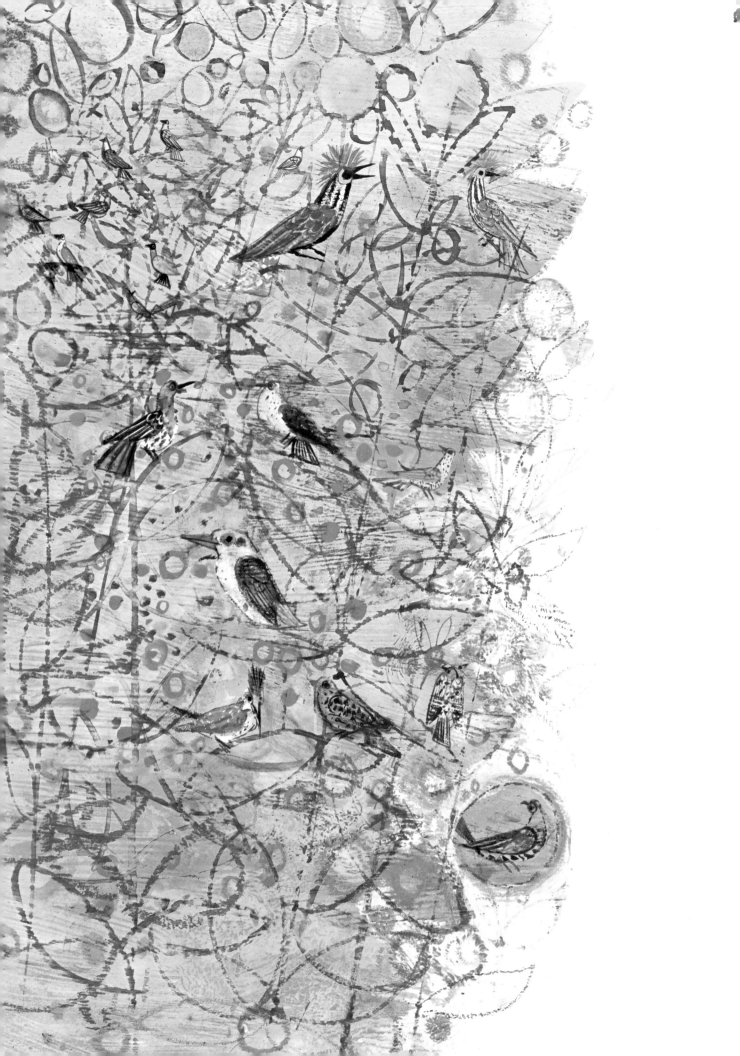

With a sigh the miller climbed down and lifted
the boy off the donkey. Wearily they plodded
along in the hot sun with the donkey trotting
gaily beside them.

At last they came to the market-place. All the
people were amused to see the miller and his
boy trudging along in the heat of the sun, when
they might have ridden on their donkey. "The
miller is crazy," they said.

The miller sold his donkey quite quickly to a
kind farmer. But his head ached from thinking
about his difficult journey and all the different
kinds of advice he had received. "From now
on," he confided to his boy, "I shall make up my
own mind and stick to it."

The boy thought this would be an excellent idea.
He nodded his head, and yawned, and they went
in search of their dinner.

Oxford University Press
Great Clarendon Street, Oxford OX2 6DP

Oxford is a registered trade mark of Oxford University Press
Copyright © Brian Wildsmith 1969
The moral rights of the author have been asserted
First published 1969 Reprinted 1970, 1972, 1975, 1980, 1984, 1986, 1987, 1990, 1992
First published in paperback 1983
All rights reserved
ISBN 0-19-272400-2
10 9 8 7 6 5 4 3 2

Printed in Hong Kong